OILY GASBAG GOES A DANCING

This novel is the first in a series of six.
With English translations for French and German
words – there are phrases in brackets within the
book and a glossary at the end.

OILY GASBAG GOES A DANCING

Written by Victor L Moore

Illustrations by Caroline Fox

Matador
Unit E2 Airfield Business Park,
Harrison Road, Market Harborough,
Leicestershire. LE16 7UL
Tel: 0116 2792299
Email: books@troubador.co.uk
Web: www.troubador.co.uk/matador
Twitter: @matadorbooks

ISBN 978 1803137 452

British Library Cataloguing in Publication Data.
A catalogue record for this book is available from the British Library.

Printed and bound by CPI Group (UK) Ltd, Croydon, CR0 4YY
Typeset in 12pt Baskerville by Troubador Publishing Ltd, Leicester, UK

Matador is an imprint of Troubador Publishing Ltd

I am especially dedicating this book to two great people, without whom my latest novel would not have been published, and to my two nephews, Aylon and Adam, and their families, as well as all my closest friends. They all know who they are.

First to my brother, Ian, whose advice and support were invaluable; and second, to my dear friend, Wilhelmina Rose, whose enthusiasm and determination to 'get Oily out there' equalled my own.

About the Author

Victor has always been fascinated by the world of fantasy and began writing short stories while at school. However, it was not until much later that he wrote his first published novel in 2013: *The Pentacle of Northumbria* – the first of a trilogy for young adults. He is also a playwright and produced a version of this very book for Mencap in 2019. His main influences are: JRR Tolkien, Lewis Carroll, CS Lewis, Philip Pullman and, for humour, PG Wodehouse – all grand wizards of the pen.

CHAPTER 1

Oily Gasbag Goes to the Fair

Nobody quite knew who or what Oily Gasbag was. The goblins denied he was of their clan. The imps shivered at the thought. The witches would curse you. The elves went into hysterics and as for the faeries, they thought you were crackers.

Oily Gasbag lived in a large toadstool, just outside the small village of Smelly-Welly, in the county of Nonsenseshire. He was very fat and his head was too big for his body. His face was marked and potted with ugly spots, and he had dark long grey hair that he never brushed. His beady eyes were bright green with bushy, dark brown eyebrows that twitched. His nose was monstrous! It was like a huge strawberry and the hairs that came out of his large nostrils wound around his nose, like wire. His mouth was thick, downturned and sneering.

He grew a straggly, untidy beard, which he rarely shaved. His ears were long, furry and pointed. He wore black trousers, held up by bright red braces, which he strapped to his various fancy shirts. His favourite was a dark blue shirt with silver stripes. He hoped that this might attract Su Fa Su Gut, the lovely elf and Beltane May Queen – fat chance! His tummy was full of the worst things you can eat and hung over his shiny black trousers, blocking out any sun, which preferred to shine on other clans. The rain, however, loved to soak him to the skin.

The remarkable thing about this crusty creature was that parts of his body could change positions. His mouth would trade places with his nose, his eyes would swap with his ears and, worst of all, his bottom would fly up and perch on his head. He had no control over his own body parts. They would move when the mood took them. He had many unpleasant habits. He would pick his nose, scratch his bottom and spit a lot.

This merry morn, on the first of May, with a shining sun, he stumbled down the hill towards the sounds and smells of the fair. He was in a good mood. All the villagers were going to the fair. It was Beltane and they wanted to see the beautiful May Queen, Su Fa Su Gut, and her band of elves and faeries dance and sing.

The fair was in the old field at the end of Lollipop Lane, the main road of the village. Here you would find

Grizzelguts, a gnarled, old pipe-smoking goblin and one of the very few friends Oily had. They were somewhat similar and few folk liked them. They would speak over each other, boasting about how great they were, while supping juice. Next door to Grizzel's shop was the imp, Crimpy Crackpot. He ran the grocery store and was small, nervous and talked very quickly. Next came La Petite Boutique ("The Little Fashion Shop") It was a posh shop and belonged to Madame Popeen Propaire. She was a French faerie, rather on the wide side, chatty but snobby. She liked neither

goblins nor imps. She particularly loathed Oily! "'E ees so rude," she would say. She preferred her own tribe and the elves, which made things a bit tricky as she still had to sell to all clans to make money.

Oily enjoyed talking, even when grumpy. He spoke in a gruff, gravelly sort of old village voice. He believed he knew about everything, when, in fact, he knew very little and often talked total nonsense. He struggled on towards the fair. It was in full swing and most of the other villagers were there, enjoying the rides, stalls and foods. It had already gone two o'clock and Oily was the last creature to arrive. He was very lazy.

Oily blundered his way over to Hattie Hasbug's Hamburger and Sausage Stall. The smell, at least to him, made his mouth water. He spat out loads of saliva.

"Oi, 'Atty! O'ill 'ave three of them sauses, two burgers – an' 'ave you gotten chips?" he shouted at her.

"Nein," she replied sharply.

"Wat youse mean 'nine'? I said three sauses an' two burgers."

"I am meaning 'nein', vich is 'no' in your English. I hef no chips," she hissed.

Hattie Hasbug hailed from Vienna in Austria and had come over to this land as a little witch girl many years ago. She was a tall, ugly, thin lady in her fifties and was the older sister of Frieda, who was the only female in town who had one eye for Oily. Unlike her sister, Hattie did not have a taste for fun and games. She was cold, grim and unfriendly. It was said that she dabbled in dark magic. However, she was a great cook and her cooking was the toast of the village.

"Why ain't youse gotten no chips then?" he bawled at her. "Oi ain't 'ad nothin' to eat since breakfast, see, an' Oi'm starvin', loike."

"Zat is not my problem," she growled. "Now, vill you be vonting your sausages?"

"Oi guess so," he snapped.

"Zat vill be sieben Schilling, bitte" ("seven shillings, please")," she demanded.

"Wot youse mean 'see Ben's marks better'?" Oily had no knowledge of German.

"Vot I mean iz, it vill cost you seven shilling," she snorted.

"Bloody pricey, if youse ask me."

5

"But novon is asking you!"

He slammed the money on the hot counter and, stuffing his huge mouth, he waddled away. Hattie sniffed but grabbed her money.

It was not a large fair, like those big American ones, but it had enough rides and stalls to cater for the needs of Smelly-Welly's unfussy folk. Oily's beady eyes swivelled around the various pleasures on view. There were five rides. First, there was the big wheel, which was rather small with only six carriages. A little way off were the dodgem cars, filled with shrieking young and nervous old. Right next door, the Dutch organ songs of the famous merry-go-round rolled out – full of happy children, riding giant chickens, crows and blackbirds. The helter skelter was the tallest. Last came the ghost train: dark and dangerous. His roving eye then caught the glare of the hall of mirrors, the coconut shy, the big slide, the candyfloss and toffee apple store, and the duck pond. It finally rested on a group of giggling elves and faeries, who were rehearsing their maypole dance.

Oily was about to shift himself to stare at the dancers, when he heard his name being yelled. Looking up, he saw his friend, Grizzelguts, on the top car of the tiny 'big' wheel.

"Oi, Oily, come an' join me – 'tis great fun up 'ere," shouted the goblin.

The wheel had stopped for a couple of imps to get out and Oily jumped into the now-empty car.

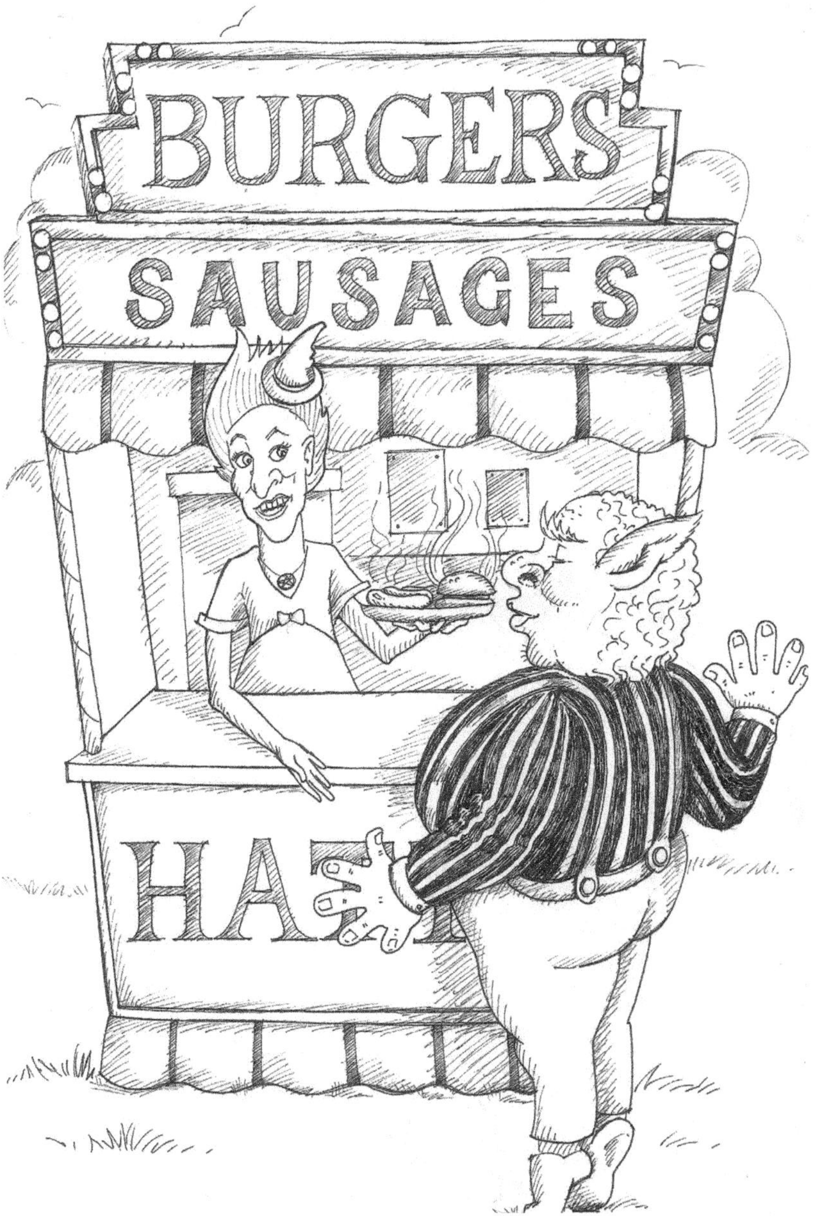
BURGERS
SAUSAGES

"That'll be three shillin', Mr Gasbag, if ye don't mind, please," demanded the voice of Miss Penny Piper, a fussy imp who was responsible for this ride. Penny Piper was a busybody and liked to think she ran the village, by poking her not-small nose into all that went on in Smelly-Welly. She was middle-aged with dark hair and very strong darting blue eyes.

"Money, money, always money," moaned Oily, as he dug deep into his pockets and produced three very grubby coins and shoved them at Penny Piper.

"Thank you, so kind!" said Penny.

Oily, now clumsily seated in his car, yelled out to his friend, "Ay, Grizzel, bet youse can't swing 'igher than me."

"Ow much then?" asked the wily goblin.

"Ten shillin'!"

"You're on, old Crocker!" shouted Grizzel.

They began to push and pull in their wooden cars to see how far each could go. The big wheel jerked and hissed, as Oily found himself swung upwards until he was on top, and Grizzel on the bottom. Grizzel was rocking away in his car, while Oily began to swing himself backwards and forwards using his arms and fat legs to make himself go even faster. Penny Piper yelled at them to stop, but they ignored her.

"Bet youse can't do that!" Oily boasted.

Just as that moment, he
lost his grip and the car sent
him flying into the air. He landed
on the roof of the dodgem cars,
before slipping through into an
unoccupied car.

"Ouch!" he yelled as he bounced up and
down in the car, as nearby folk giggled away.

"Ain't nothin' ter laugh at," he bellowed, as four
dodgem cars, with shrieking young witches, headed
directly for him. As they crashed into him, off he
flew again, before landing slap bang into the young
elves and faeries rehearsing their maypole dance.
They shrieked and fled. He grasped the maypole and
brought it down on top of him.

"You silly old fool! You ef ruined our dancing," screamed Madame Popeen Propaire, who was helping the younger elves and faeries, most of whom had scattered away in fright.

"No, Oi ain't," he yelled back. "T'were them stoopid young witches' fault on them dodgy cars. They wents for me, see. Friends of yourn, no doubt!"

"You are a 'orrible creature; zis is what I sink."

"Oi don't give no fig what youse 'sink'. Oi ain't no ship. Go and chop chips."

"What a rude creature, eh?" she sniffed, as she stormed off to help the elves and faeries put the maypole up again.

Oily plonked his big bottom on the grass and watched as the pretty creatures huffed and puffed working hard to get the pole straight again. He was much too lazy to offer his help, which only would have made matters worse. As he lay idly on the bright green grass, Grizzelguts shuffled over to join him.

"Where's me ten shillin' then?" Oily demanded.

"You'll be lucky, me old pal," sneered the goblin.

"Wot youse mean 'lucky'? Oi beats yer fair an' square," snarled Oily.

"Aye, you did beat the fair, for sure," he laughed, "but 't'were me what won, cos unlike you, I stayed in me car, see."

"That still don't make youse the winner."

"Oh aye, it do."

"No, it don't."

"*It do!*" screamed Grizzelguts, as both stood glaring at each other.

"*It don't!*" roared Oily, in his friend's ear.

The two creatures were getting very cross with each other. Neither was aware that not only had Su Fa Su Gut and Madame Popeen Propaire got the pole upright again, but they had begun the famous maypole dance for Beltane. All rides and stalls were at a standstill, as the village folk now rushed over to see the pretty elves and faeries dance and sing. The two clans were whirling around the maypole, skipping and screaming in joy, as a small band of goblins and imps began to play their flutes, violins and drums. The faeries and elves, all with lovely garlands in their long hair, passed over and under each other, enjoying every moment, as they danced and pranced around the maypole, making a large ring.

The dancing stopped; into the middle of the ring came a pretty young elf. She was about to sing a love song. This was the beautiful Su Fa Su Gut. She cleared her throat and began to sing a well-known old folk song, 'She Moves Through The Fair'. As soon as Oily heard her voice, he stopped arguing with Grizzel and pushed his way through the small crowd to the front. Ignoring everyone, he stared at Su Fa, like a love-struck schoolboy.

As she finished her song to great cheering, the dancing began again and Oily Gasbag decided to join in. The lovely young things were laughing away as they whirled and twirled around each other and the maypole. The Goblin and Imp Band were playing their flutes and violins at full blast. Su Fa Su Gut was leading the rest, going from one to the other as she touched the hand of one elf before moving on to a faerie, and so on. Just as she was about to sing the second verse of the famous old folk song, Oily arrived. He barged a fumbling faerie out of the way and went to seize Su Fa's hand. Su Fa was so shocked that she stood still and all the rest just fell into each other, with most falling over.

"Oi luvs yer," he growled at her. She just stared at

him, unable to speak. The band, however, continued to play. None of this seemed to worry Oily. Having grabbed Su Fa's hand, he tried to spin her round. Now, she woke up. She took one look at this ugly, stupid creature, who had ruined her dance and her day, and gripping him with a mighty clasp (which for a young elf was remarkable), she hurled him into the crowd of grim-looking onlookers.

Oily tried to get to his feet as angry folk pounced on him. As he shouted and yelled, three large goblins and two witches marched him to the edge of the field, where one of the goblins kicked him out of the fair and back onto the dusty road.

"And don't ye come back," they screamed at him.

"Oi'll get youse. Youse see if Oi don't," he shouted back.

Oily was angry. He was muddy. He was dirty. He shook a big hairy fist at the laughing crowd, which included his friend, Grizzelguts. He sighed and headed wearily back to his toadstool home, muttering oaths all the way.

CHAPTER 2

Oily Gasbag Tries to Dance

Oily went to bed that night in a very angry mood. When he woke up the next morning, he was even angrier. It was hot. He yawned, showing the gaps in his yellow teeth. He stretched, spat on his dirty toadstool floor – once white, but now grey – and stumbled out of bed.

He dressed himself, forgetting to wash or, indeed, brush his teeth, and went into his messy kitchen, which was next door to his bedroom, and made himself a cup of dirty-brown tea. He helped himself to stale biscuits and munched and slurped. He scratched his bottom and picked up a stubby pencil from his old wobbly wooden kitchen table and stuffed it into his ear to clean dirty wax. He fumbled around in a drawer and pulled out a few torn pages from a tatty old directory for services of magical folk. He squinted over the pages until he found what he was looking for.

"That'll do for starters," he muttered to himself.

He roughly scrawled around three names that caught his bulging green eyes. The first name he spotted was:

Faerie Footsteps.
Come et learn 'ow to be light on your feets
and dance so sweet au Faerie Footsteps.
Contact Faerie La France in Lollipop Lane.

"Ain't far ter go there, then," he told himself. The second name was 'Striktly Goblin'. Here, they informed the ignorant reader:

Striktly Goblin will teach you how to dance better than
any other clan or your money back guaranteed.

The address was given as Raspberry Road. "Oi'll ask for me money back there," chortled the measly creature. The third advert was the star turn, as far as Oily was concerned. It simply said:

Can't dance? Can't meet your dream partner? Five
lessons with us and you will be the most sought-after
creature in Smelly-Welly. Please call or visit Die
Hexen von Wanderlust at the top of Lemon Sherbet
Hill.

Mm, like the sound of that, but a flippin' long way to walk, thought Oily. After arguing loudly with himself, laziness won the day. He decided to stroll down the road to Faerie Footsteps. He was such a dim-witted fellow that he failed to realise that the address given was upstairs at Madame Popeen Propaire's La Petite Boutique. He marched into her shop in his big dirty boots, leaving traces of mud all over her dark mauve carpet. Madame Popeen Propaire was busy fussing over a customer, a snooty faerie, who was trying on hats that were far too big for her. Her name was Lilly Lally and she was tiny compared to Madame, but like the French faerie, she was very snobbish.

"Oi you, Oi wanna know where to find that Francis Faerie, wot teaches blokes loike me ter dance. 'As a room 'ere, so it says, in this 'ere paper."

Madame Popeen Propaire spun round, her eyes blazing at the sight of this ugly creature ruining her plush carpet.

"Vous! Quitte ma boutique, maintenant!" ("You! Get out of my shop, now!") she screamed at him in French. He had no idea what she was saying, but even he could see that this was one furious faerie.

Fuming, she retorted to a funny mix of English and French. "Out you go, now, comprenez vous?" ("do you understand?")

"Oi wanna knows where to find this Francis woman wot teaches dance, like it sez 'ere," he yelled back at her.

"Imbecile! C'est moi!" ("Idiot! It is me!")

"Wot youse on about, yer daft faerie?"

"You stupide fool. It is I 'oo teaches la dance, but no for you. You breeng in you mess, you very rude an' I srow you out my shop."

"'Elp me, s'il vous plaît ("if you please"), Lilly Lally."

"Pleasure be," replied Lilly Lally.

Together, the two faeries managed to propel the spluttering Oily out into the street.

"And you never come backs to my shop. Jamais! Allez!" ("Never! Go!")

"Smelly old thing, I want to wash my hands after touching that creature," sniffed Lilly Lally.

"And zat iz zat," cried Madame Popeen Propaire, rubbing her chubby hands.

For the second time in under a day, Oily Gasbag dusted himself off. His bottom was getting very sore. He placed his ugly face to the window of the dress shop and banged his huge hairy fist on the window. The two faeries were so busy nattering about hats and things that they did not even notice him.

"Flamin' faeries! Wot they know about dancin' anyway?" he swore.

Luckily for Oily, Raspberry Avenue was but a short hop from Lollipop Lane. He peered in the doorway of his old mate, Grizzelguts, only to find it was without goblins, or any other clan for that matter.

A message written in Grizzel's spidery hand informed all would-be bread buyers:

AINT WERKIN TERDAY CUM BAK
TERMORER KLOZED.

Short and to the point, despite the spelling. Chuckling to himself, Oily shambled along Lollipop Lane, until he came to a small, cobbled road. He turned left and, within a minute, he arrived outside a ramshackle building with a blue light over its door, which itself was hanging on its hinges. The sign read:

STRIKTLY GOBLIN SKOOL OV DANZ.

He entered the shop. The ground floor was deserted, but above he heard weird music and clomping. Walking up the shaky staircase, Oily came to a large untidy room, with dirty grey wooden floor panels, where the dark green and stinking walls had nasty yellow wallpaper peeling away. It was stuffy. There was one small filthy window and you could barely see the street below. In the centre of the room stood a huge old gramophone on which a whistling and cracking record was hissing out a sort of large banging sound, to which four goblins were attempting to dance.

Oily knew them all. His old mate, Grizzelguts, was winding up a machine. Standing next to him, a big fat smile on her spotted face, was Scrumbletops – a large, loping goblin, with squirty green eyes, snout nose and a greedy mouth. She was the nearest thing to a girlfriend for Grizzelguts. Despite his lack of affection for her, she still liked him. Over in the corner stood another couple. They were Ho Ho He and Ha Ha She. They were married. Unlike so many of their

clan, they liked to have fun and were huge jokers.
They were the owners of this odd shop and ran the
dance classes. Again, Oily should have guessed this,
but of course he did not.

"Oh, it's youse two wot runs this dance thing,
then?" asked Oily.

"Guilty as charged, ole Mr Gasbag," chirped Ha Ha She.

"Don't youse call me old, see," he snorted.

"Why not? You is old, very old, ain't 'e, Ho Ho?" she giggled, as she nudged her husband.

"It's only a bit of fun, Oily. Stop growlin' like a bloomin' bear."

Oily decided to ignore their silly comments and turning to his best mate, he asked, "Wot you doin' 'ere then?"

"Wot's it look like?" Grizzel replied.

"Oi dunno! Youse playin' that thing then or dancin'?"

"Both!"

"E's a great dancer, me Grizzel, ain't yer, me darlin'?" exclaimed Scrumbletops.

"If 'e's so great, why's 'e 'avin lessons then?" asked a smirking Oily.

"Cos I'm teachin' 'im, see!"

"You! Youse couldn't teach a monkey to crack nuts," Oily laughed.

"It ain't monkeys wot crack nuts, it's parrots, you silly old berk," growled Scrumbletops. There was no love lost between Oily and his best pal's girlfriend.

"So 'oo's gonna dance with me?" Oily demanded.

"S'ppose it'll have to be me," sighed Ha Ha She.

"Make sure 'e don't tread on your feet, me love," joked Ho Ho He.

"Youse can shut yer big gob an' all," shouted Oily.

"Charmin'! And wot about payin' us, then? We ain't doin' this for fun, ye know," said Ho Ho He.

"It says 'ere, in this advert, that youse gets your money back," Oily grunted.

"Right, but we gotta see your silver first, like!"

"'Ow much then?"

"Twenty shillin', if ye please, kind sir," grinned Ha Ha She.

"Youse gotta be jokin'," groaned Oily.

"That be the price; take it or leave it," she snarled.

"Ain't got it, see," he yelled. Oily had not given any thought to bringing money. He just did not think ahead. Besides, he was mean and greedy. So, it came as a real surprise when his old mate, Grizzelguts, decided to shelve out for him.

"I'll pay for 'im. 'E can't 'elp bein' mean. That's the way he be, see," smiled Grizzel.

"Wot youse do that for?" Oily demanded to know, without a word of thanks to his old mate.

"I 'ave me reasons, see," he replied with a mysterious wink to the others, which Oily failed to see.

"Well, orrite then. But if it don't work, Oi wants me money back, loike it says 'ere."

"Your money! You mean mine, you miserable ole goat…"

Ho Ho stepped in between the two angry creatures. "We're all 'ere to dance, see, not fight."

The two 'friends' grunted but no more was said,

and Olly Gasbag began his first ever dancing lesson. It did not start well. They had all been trying to learn an old goblin folk dance. This was like formation dancing with partners, bowing then moving towards each other. The woman then skips around the man and then they link arms and dance past each other. The woman then goes to the next man and the whole dance repeats itself. Quite simple, really – only it wasn't for Oily Gasbag. Whether he was too eager, too rough or too stupid, probably a mix of three, was difficult to say.

The other three all bowed to each other; Oily did not. Perhaps Ha Ha She should have explained that to Oily, but she chose not to. He then remained still, as Grizzelguts danced towards Scrumbletops and they met in the middle. Both females then skipped around their male partners, then Grizzel and Scrumbletops linked hands and skipped towards Oily and Ha Ha She. This was where Oily should have linked hands with Ha Ha and danced in the opposite direction, so that the two couples would pass each other. Instead of allowing her to link hands with him, however, Oily grabbed her by her large waist and with his clumsy, clumpy arms, he spun her round so fast that she lost her balance and fell to the floor, with Oily collapsing on top of her. She was not best pleased.

"Get off me, you stupid oaf," she yelled.

Grizzel and Ho Ho were only too willing to pull Oily away, which they did with great joy, picking him

up and flinging him to the wall, where he again fell to the floor, with shrieking laughter ringing in his big ears.

Ha Ha picked herself up. She brushed away all the dust and muck that wanted to remain stuck to her shiny face. "Dance! You couldn't dance with a pig or cow, Oily Gasbag! They both would dance rings around you," she screeched at him.

Oily got up. He was dishevelled, dusty and extremely angry. "Call that teachin'? Youse couldn't teach a pig ter dance," he snarled at her.

"I could teach a blind cat ter dance better than you. Give 'im 'is money back, luv, an' throw 'im out," she told her grinning hubby.

The greedy figure held out his hand. He was about to get another shock.

"If you remember loike, it were yer ole mate, Grizzelguts, wot paid for you, so unless you want me boot up your backside, I suggest you take that fat frame o' yourn out o' our shop. I don't take kindly to folk like you, treating me good lady like that," stormed Ho Ho.

"Wot youse on about? It were your ruddy lady wot was not teachin' me right, see, an… an…"

Oily Gasbag had worked himself up to such a point that his mouth and nose started to twitch and quiver and, amid howls of laughter, they swapped places.

"Oi'll shows youse all. Youse see if… erm… gurb erk ouch," he mumbled – but with his mouth now where his nose was and his nose replacing his mouth, it all came out very jumbled. The other four could not stop laughing. Oily did not need an escort to show him the exit door. Cursing away with his nose spraying showers of snot in all directions, he stumbled down the stairs and out of the shop and back into the street. His second attempt to learn to dance had been even more disastrous than his first. He could still hear their hysterical shrieks as he shambled away.

There was now only one choice left for our grumbling goblin-like creature and that was a long, uphill walk to Die Hexen von Wanderlust ("The Witches Who Like to Wander"), but being lazy, Oily did not fancy a long walk, so he decided to wait for the village bus.

27

The local bus service was run by Inky Iddlewot, a moody imp, who would only take his precious bus out when he fancied it, and only pick up and drop off passengers if he liked them.

For once in his life, Oily was in luck. The rickety old bus approached, chugging along the cobbled road. Inky realised who it was, who had put his grubby hand out and swerved to avoid picking up Oily. The fussy imp did not want him on his bus – but he was to have no choice in the matter.

Oily, by now fuming, went to stand in the very middle of the road, forcing Inky to slam on his creaky brake. Much as disliked Oily, he did not want to run him over – but it was not only that. Sitting in the back of the bus were a bunch of young witches, who were giggling away and very much wanted Oily to join them for their own rather silly and selfish reasons. The bus halted and the lumbering creature clambered aboard.

"Don't you go a makin' a mess on my luverly bus, 'ere, or you goes straight off, Mister Gasbag," was Inky's not-very-nice greeting.

"Gobe blab yot het in ale," Oily snorted, spraying snot over the seats. What he was trying to tell the stuffy Inky was, "Go boil your head in oil."

The four young witches pleaded with Inky to let Oily stay and even offered to pay his fare, which was only one shilling. The four were the only other passengers on the bus and Inky reluctantly took the shilling coin from the eldest witch, who was Caramel Cathy. Her three friends were Selina Snakebite, Paula Prune and Natalie Nastie. While not evil, they were very mischievous and when they chose to, they could be right little devils.

Oily grunted something and Inky shrugged his neat little shoulders, and the bus began the long climb up the road to Lemon Sherbet Hill. This was the part of the village where nearly all the witches and wizards had their beautiful magical houses, of which they were very proud. They lived at the very top of the village and believed that they were the best of all the various clans. Maybe they were, maybe not. One thing was for sure. They knew more about magic than any other tribe and how best to use it — and not always for the right reasons.

"Hey, Mistah Gosbag! Aye, we mean ye, why not join us at the back o' the bus?" requested Caramel Cathy.

"Oh yes, do come and sit wi' us. Ye bein' such a fine gentleman now," added Selina Snakebite, while Paula Prune and Natalie Nastie just sniggered.

"Grite," was all Oily managed. He was trying to say 'alright'. He even tried to smile, but his mouth, being where his nose ought to have been, was turned upside down, so it seemed as if he was sneering at everyone, which was not far from his usual look, of course.

Oily shuffled over to the four grinning, naughty, young witches and placed his huge bottom on the two seats in front of them. His bottom being so wide, he needed both seats to feel comfortable. This would often cause rows with other passengers, who did not want him to sit anywhere near them, let alone next to them.

"Ain't 'e 'andsome?" laughed Paula Prune.

"'E be one o' the most 'andsome men in our village, do ye not think so, girls?" Selina Snakebite smirked.

"Do ye 'ear that, Mistah Dustbog? Me an' me good friends all be thinkin' ye be some catch now," cackled Natalie Nastie.

"And don't be forgettin' 'is manners now. Why, me own grannie, Old Mother Nochops – BLESSED BE to 'er – well, she says, says she, that she never be 'earin' such manners now, girls," giggled Caramel Cathy.

Poor old Oily. He was so keen to speak and remind them that his name was not Mistah Dustbog, but the words would just not come.

"Urrg nsum Gsbrag," was his best effort. But this just sent these wicked witches into shrieks of laughter. The silly creature really did believe that these awful young witches actually liked him, which made his huge head swell with pride.

"Can't ye talk proper, Mistah Crossgag?" asked the cheeky Selinda Snakebite. Oily gallantly tried to talk again, but his efforts only produced more snot and redder, uglier lips. He was blowing so hard and

going so red in the face that it looked as if he would explode at any moment.

Inky Iddlewot could have warned Oily that these girls were poking fun at him, but he was enjoying seeing Oily unable to talk properly with his face in such a mess, so he just chortled quietly to himself and allowed the giggling girls to carry on.

"Oh, look at 'im now. Poor creature. What wi' 'is mouth an' 'is nose a swappin' over, like, 'tis no wonder 'e can't talk proper, see, girls," said Caramel Cathy.

"We could 'elp im, though, girls, could we not? After all, young witches do we be, and spells do we make for all to see," suggested the sly Selinda Snakebite, with a twinkling wink to the other three.

"'Course we could, girls. I've me wand wi' me an' you all got yours, then?" Caramel Cathy asked her friends.

"Aye, we do," they chorused.

"Don't you girls go a making mischief on my bus now," shouted a worried Inky.

"As if we would be a doing such a thing now, Mistah Idiot. We only be a wantin' to help poor, old – that be very old – Mistah Glassbig, now, be that so, girls?"

"Oh, that be so," the other three chortled.

"Alright then, but mind no nonsense now. And by the way, me name is Inky Iddlewot, not Idiot, see!"

"'Course 'tis. Silly me, now," said Caramel Cathy.

"Right then, girls. Wands out!" ordered Caramel Cathy, who was the leader of their small gang.

Each witch produced her wand. Two were coloured red; two were shaded purple.

"Dear, dear ole Mistah Fusshag, we lovely-looking young witches be going to make ye look 'andsome again, ain't we, girls?" smiled Caramel Cathy.

"Oh, for sure," they replied, all grinning.

Each witch held her wand up high. "Now, on count o' three, repeat after me," ordered Caramel Cathy.

"One, two, three. Oh, Mistah Wasstag, how happy ye will be, when we bring back a smile to ye face, that be full o' misery. Your huge fat nose, go back in place, just like a raspberry. As for your mouth, from north to south, grow larger, so shall ye!"

The four of them were giggling so much, they could barely cast their spell. But cast it they did, and after some blue and black smoke, Oily was almost himself again. Almost, but not quite. He could talk again, but his mouth was now twice its normal size and his nose was now the shape of a large, dark red raspberry. To make matters worse, he had become much bigger and fatter! He nearly turned Inky's bus over, so large had he become. It finally dawned on him that these nasty little girls were having fun at his expense. He shook his huge fist at them. He snarled, he growled, he groaned, he yelled. The bus stopped. Inky ordered him off and asked the willing witches to help him. They did so, screeching with laughter.

He was still only halfway up the hill. He just caught a glance of the four shrieking witches at the back of the bus, poking their pierced tongues out at him as the old bus creaked its way up the hill. Oily shook his huge head and wandered his way homeward. His trip, to what he still thought would be his best choice to learn to dance, would now have to wait until another day.

CHAPTER 3

Frieda Pays Oily a Flying Visit

Oily returned to his toadstool home. He was tired. He was upset. He spat and cursed. He kicked out at his ancient rickety chair.

"Bloomin' chair, wicked witches, fat faeries, daft imps an' gobby goblins. Oi'll gets me own back on all of yers, youse sees if Oi doesn't," he screeched at the top of his voice, terrifying a large black cat that had wandered into his messy kitchen, only to scuttle out again.

He tried to cook himself some lunch. This, too, was not very good. He was now so large and clumsy that everything he did went wrong. He burnt his egg and beans and nearly blew up his iron stove while cooking chips that were drenched in oil – even Oily could not eat them. He was so weary that he fell asleep in his old chair and his loud snores echoed fiercely, scaring away all other forms of animals and folk. It was said that when Oily Gasbag snored after eating, it could be heard all over Smelly-Welly, and the good citizens had to put cottonwool in their ears to muffle the sound.

He was in the middle of a wonderful dream, where he was chasing witches, imps, faeries and goblins into the sea, when he felt he was being shaken and woke up. There, standing in front of him, with a hideous grin, was his so-called girlfriend and the only creature, apart from Grizzelguts, who liked him.

"Wot youse doin' 'ere? 'Ow youse got in me 'ouse then?" he grumbled.

"Is zis der vay you speak mit deine liebe freundin, ja?" ("your lovely girlfriend, yes?") the other smiled back.

"Wot youse want, anyway?" he snarled at her.

"I am here for helping you, meine gut friend. I am hearing zat, die jungen Hexen ("the young witches") be making – 'ow you zay in English – der joke, ja, und I am zinking zat ve make zem pay, ja?"

"Oh, right. Oi sees. Well, that's a bit different then. Wot's 'dee young on hexhen' mean, then?"

"Ha ha! Das ist German for 'ze young vitches'. Zey make fun of you on der bus an' I am not likin' zis. Zey machen spass mit Magie ("make fun with magic"), zo ve make bad for zem, ja?"

"Oi loikes that." Oily smiled for the first time since his misadventures.

Hattie Hasbug's younger sister, Frieda, returned his smile. Her eyes were glimmering with gleeful trickery.

"First ve make you vot you vere. Avay mit der grosse head," she shouted, producing a large black wand that she frantically waved around Oily's musty kitchen. Sparks flew hither and thither. Purple and black smoke rose from the floor, making both Frieda and Oily cough. But it did the trick. In less than a minute, Oily's size was reduced to normal – that is, normal for Oily. Anyway, he seemed content. He almost thanked Frieda, but said nothing apart from a brief nod in her direction. And that was enough for her.

"Zo, ve start, ja. Ve needing to make zer plan, ich denke, ja ("I think, yes")," she told him as she

beckoned him with a long pointy finger to sit. He sat
on his old chair.

Frieda then conjured up a very comfy chair with
a cushion and sat opposite him. "Vot vould you like
to do, zo ve make zem feel bad, ja?" she asked him,
with an evil grin.

"Dunno!' Make 'em all disappear for ever, see,"
he snarled. He was not very bright.

"Zat, I can't make. But I hef a gut plan, zat I zink
very much you vill like, Oily," she replied.

"Wot is it then? Better be bloody good an 'all,"
he snorted, showing his ignorance of the wonderful
magic of Austrian witchcraft.

"Vot if I told you zat zere iz a dancing competition
at ze vitches coven tomorrow and you and I – ve
going to vin!"

"'Ow youse goin' to be doin' that then?"

"Mit magic, of course… und, vell, let's say a bit of cheating, ja?"

Oily's eyes lit up. "Can't wait. Let's show 'em!" he smirked.

"I knew you could like mein idea," she grinned back at him.

Then, he frowned again. "But Oi can't dance… that's why Oi wanted ter learn 'ow, see, an' all them stopped…"

"You don't hef to. You can leave all zat to me," laughed Frieda.

"Wat youse mean?" asked the baffled Oily.

"I am von clever vitch. I make mit all sorts of magic."

"But Oi don't—" began the worried creature.

Frieda cut him off. "No more mit der qvestions, please. All you hef to do is follow me. Even you can do zat, I am zinking, no?"

"Oi suppose so," grunted Oily. Much as he wanted to get his own back on nearly all the folk of the village, he did not want to be bossed about by this cheeky Austrian witch. But he knew deep down – in his smelly old boots – that if he really wanted to show them all up, then he had no choice but to follow Frieda's lead. He sighed, snorted and nodded.

"Wunderbar!" ("Wonderful!") gasped Frieda. "Now ve make our plans, ja?"

She informed him that he would have to

come back with her to her home, Die Hexen von Wanderlust, at the very top of Lemon Sherbet Hill.

Oily scowled. "'Tis too bloomin' long to walk, see, an' Oi'm tired," he grumbled.

"Zere vill be no valking. You ride mit me on mein Besenstiel, nein?" ("my broomstick, no?") chuckled Frieda.

"Your watta?" exclaimed Oily.

"Vot you say in your English is 'my broomstick'!"

"Well, speaks in Ingerlish then, yer daft Orstrine witch," moaned Oily. Being rude came more easily to him than being polite.

"Und zis is der zanks I am getting, ja," she snorted, tossing back her flaxen curly hair.

"This 'ere is Ingerland, see, an' Oi don't un'erstan' Orstrine, loike!"

If this was the best she was going to get for an apology, Frieda knew better than to start a row with the grumpy, goblin-like creature. Smiling, she informed him, "Is not Austrian, but German. I am from Wien in Austria, but zere, like all in mein country, ve speak Deutsch – I am meaning German!"

"Don't care where youse been weaned; 'ere we speaks Ingerlish, proper loike, see," retorted Oily.

Frieda was about to tell her idiot of a 'boyfriend' that 'Wien', pronounced 'Veen', was German for 'Vienna', the capital of Austria, from where both she and her miserable sister hailed. She thought better of it. It would only make him more confused and annoyed, so she said no more on the subject.

"Now, you must, mit me, come back to der vitches homes for ve hef to do some practising… if you vont to vin. Und, you do vont to vin, don't you, mein guter Mann ("my good man")?"

"'Course Oi wanna win, don't talk stoopid!"

"In zat case, on mit my Besenstiel and off ve fly, zen!"

Without fully realising what was happening to him, Oily found himself on an old wooden broomstick, sitting behind Frieda. He heard a mewing sound and turned to see a large, black cat sneering at him, as it settled down at the end of the flying broom. This was Frieda's cat, Greetagrach; he had scared her off and she glared at him, her green eyes aglow.

It did not take long for the ancient Austrian broomstick to reach the part of the village known as Die Hexen Wunder Platz, which in English meant The Witches Place of Wonder. It was so called because many years ago, when the very early ancestors had come from Saxony in Germany and parts of the Austrian Alps, they had settled at the top of the hill in Smelly-Welly, which used to be called Klein Wein, meaning Little Vienna; but the other newer and larger folk, such as goblins, imps and faeries, had protested, so they renamed it Smelly-Welly, due to the peculiar smells that would come up over the morning mists when the old farmers and milkmaids would return from their daily chores with dirty, stinking mud and other things on their boots. The folk back then made up the funny name and it stuck – as did the mud! But the ancient Saxony folk insisted that their part of the village still be in German and it was agreed to call it Die Hexen Wunder Platz, which it has been since.

Frieda Hasbug lived in a tumbledown cottage on the edge of the woods, which she shared with her rather nasty sister, Hattie. Both had their special rooms, so only usually met for meals as Frieda could not cook a bean without magic, while Hattie could conjure up great food in an instant without the use of spells. Their cottage was covered in fern, weeds and dark branches, which, if you were not careful, would reach out and trap you, and not let you go!

Frieda's room was a muddled mess of broken stools, flying chairs, old oak tables that sometimes spoke, large books of magic, spilled spells, coloured lotions, weird potions and a huge picture of Vienna, and one other picture of her and her sister when they were children. The walls were purple, the ceiling red and the floor was covered with a bright green carpet, which sparked from time to time. Messy it may have been, but it had a magical charm of its very own. This was not the first time that Oily had been invited to the sisters' cottage. He was not comfortable there, as he never knew what might happen next.

"Vould you like to drink zumzink, Oily?" Frieda asked him, in a soft voice.

Oily glanced nervously around the room. "Wot youse got then?" he enquired.

"I hef here, for you, a very special drink, vitch I zink vill make you relax und feel easy – ja, mein Freund ("yes, my friend"). You are looking very vorried, so you drink zis und all your vorries, zey go avay, ja?"

She laughed and poured out a very odd-looking green liquid from one of her glass cones. She then added another potion, which was yellow and shook the glass until the two potions mixed, giving off a smell of aniseed and showing a brownish colour. Oily hesitated, but after a bossy stare from Frieda, he took his courage in both hands and greedily slurped the mixture down in two gulps, with Frieda watching closely. Oily tried to speak but found the room was spinning and his big head dropped into his lap. He was not snoring, but he was in a deep sleep.

"Das ist gut ("This is good"). Now I hef him vere I vont him," cackled Frieda and skipped out of the room to tell her awful sister what she had just done!

CHAPTER 4

The Hasbug Sisters' Dancing Spell

It was not very often that Frieda wanted to talk to her grim sister, but she could not wait to tell her about Oily. This would both annoy and amuse Hattie. She ran into their kitchen, where Hattie was cooking a tasty lunch from Austria: Vienna schnitzel! She was busy stirring her cauldron with a large wooden spoon, so did not see her sister creep up on her. Hattie was throwing all sorts of scrumptious bits and pieces into the bubbling cauldron as she hummed an old Viennese song to herself. She missed the old city and often wished she could return there – if not for ever, at least for a visit.

"Hattie, Hattie, kommst du mit mir, bitte ("come with me, please")," she yelled in her sister's ear.

Hattie turned around. She was not pleased. She hated it when others talked to her when she was cooking. She did not like talking nor listening to folk, anyway.

"Warum? Was willst du?" ("Why? What do you want?") she snarled, glaring at Frieda.

"Wir haben einen Gast." ("We have a guest.")

"Einen Gast! Wie?" ("A guest! Who?")

"Est ist mein guter Freund, Oily Gasbag!" ("It is my good friend, Oily Gasbag!")

"Was? Dieser Dummkopf!" ("What? That idiot!")

Frieda went into a long explanation – in German, of course – as to why she had brought one of her sister's least favourite folk into their pretty, but private cottage. Hattie was frowning and sneering at first, but bit by bit, as the excited Frieda laid out her crazy plan in front of her, a smile lit up her sour mouth. When her sister finally finished, Hattie gazed at her in admiration and allowed herself a little laugh.

"Er schläfts jetzt?" ("He is sleeping now?")

The sisters came into Frieda's room and the sight that greeted them was not pleasant. Oily was slumped in a wicker chair, his huge mouth wide open, showing his ugly, yellow teeth – well, that is, the few that were still there! He was now snoring heavily and it shook the walls. Hattie wanted to go over to the ugly creature and kick him in the foot, but Frieda stopped her. She went over to him and shook him, perhaps not as gently as before.

He stirred. He opened his eyes, blinked, coughed, looked at Frieda, then stared at Hattie, who glared back, and spluttered, "Wot she doin' ere?"

"I live here, you dummkopf," Hattie growled.

"Oi'm 'ungry! Wot youse got to eat, then?"

"Hattie and I are making for you a very nice meal, vitch you vill like, please," explained Frieda.

"Wot's in it then?" came the ungrateful reply.

"Frogs, toads, snails and vasps mit fried ants, you stupid creature," yelled Hattie.

"Youse is an ugly, old—" began Oily.

Before Oily and her sister came to blows, Frieda put a stop to any more rows between them. "Stille, bitte!" ("Quiet, please!") she shouted. "Listen to me! You vont for us to vin dieser Tanz ("this dance"), yes?"

"Natürlch, ja!" snapped Hattie. ("Of course, yes!")

"S'ppose so," Oily muttered.

"Gut, zat is good. Zis is vot ve are doing zen."

In easy words, which even a daft creature like Oily could understand, Frieda explained how they were going to win the dance competition. Hattie was going to cook a wonderful meal of Austrian delight and Frieda would sprinkle some dark magic potions that would turn her into the queen of dance. If Oily followed her lead, then he, too, would become a very good dancer. That was, of course, as long as the spell worked. She told him almost everything. What she did not tell him was that the Hexen Volk had decided that the winning couple would visit Vienna for a long weekend and go to the grandest ball of all at the Wiener Konzerthaus. Hattie had only agreed to this devious plan if Frieda took her and left that awful creature behind. Frieda had no choice, because like her sister, she, too, desperately wanted to win and return to the city of her childhood.

The three of them went into the huge kitchen and sat down to a gorgeous feast of Viennese schnitzel, sausages, potato dumplings and cabbage, followed by a beautiful Viennese cake with ice cream. For once, Oily was so busy stuffing himself that he spoke no words, while the sisters exchanged mischievous smiles. Hattie barely hid her disgust at the way Oily shovelled down his food, burping and belching after each huge bite. Frieda, however, was happy to see him gobbling like a pig, because the faster he ate, the greater the spell would be.

"That were real good," he bellowed, as Hattie sniffed and Frieda giggled.

"You must zank Hattie, Oily, for it is she vot made ze cooking und me vot put in ze magic," said Frieda.

"Yea, right," was all Hattie got in thanks.

"Now ve see if

48

a big, fat creature like you can dance, ja?" Hattie snorted.

"Now ve play ze music and see if ze magic vorks, ja?" Frieda suggested.

"But Oi've just eaten," Oily protested.

"No matter, ve dance now," shouted Frieda as she forced Oily out of his comfy chair, much to the delight of her sister.

"I play ze waltz on mein violin, and you and him, dance," grinned Hattie.

Poor old Oily had no choice. He wanted to sleep after such a meal, but the sisters had other ideas. Together, they rushed him to his feet, and Frieda made him put his heavy arms around her waist and went to place her dainty hand on his bulging shoulder. Hattie picked up an old violin and began to play a grand waltz. Oily, led by Frieda, began to dance. Oily surprised himself. At first, Frieda waltzed him around the kitchen, which, with its tables, chairs, oven and saucepans, was perhaps not the best place to learn to dance, so he was all over the place. He bumped into the table, knocked down two of the chairs and nearly squeezed the life out of Frieda, with his heavy arm around her waist.

As Hattie, playing her violin with a superior scowl on her unattractive face, brought the charm of Viennese music into their home, Frieda managed to do the impossible. She taught Oily how to waltz! Slowly, he lost his clumsiness and found his feet were dancing in time to the strings of one of the great Austrian waltzes. He was no longer treading on Frieda's feet. His movements, which up to now had had the grace of an uninvited prancing hippopotamus at a posh tea party, changed. Not only was he dancing in time to Strauss, but he was also dancing in step with the delighted Frieda. She smiled at him and, for the first time ever in their relationship, he grinned back.

"Das its gut, Oily," ("This is good") she beamed at him.

"Oi is a gettin' the 'ang of it, ain't Oi?"

He was. He had forgotten that this was really the work of magical food and potions, which had turned him from a clumsy oaf into a waltzing wonder. Hattie reminded him.

"It iz not you but ze magic vot is making you gut," she told him as the waltz ended.

"Don't care, see," was his childish response. The snooty Austrian witch was not expecting that. She sniffed, stuck her nose up in the air, but said no more, for which Frieda was secretly grateful.

The trio spent the next hour dancing and playing the violin to a variety of waltzes. Oily was getting cocky. He thought he was the king of dance. He was not. When the magic wore off, he would again become the clumsy clot he always had been. But for now, he felt important. After a few more waltzes, Frieda introduced him to the polka, cha-cha, foxtrot and quickstep, and he managed to dance the lot with flying colours. Even the grim-faced Hattie was impressed, but she had her own reasons for wanting her sister to win, of which Oily knew nothing.

CHAPTER 5

Waltzing into Vienna?

Somehow, probably with a mix of magic and madness, Frieda persuaded Oily to stay overnight at their lovely little cottage, as it was the eve of the dance competition. She told him that he needed to be there to get a good night's sleep, but there was one condition that Hattie had insisted on. He had to have a bath, otherwise the deal was off. Oily did not like water, except to drink it. He took great pride and effort in being smelly, but was given little choice. If he refused, it was back to his home, with no chance of getting his own back on all his enemies, which were most of Smelly-Welly.

So, having tossed and turned all night, in the sisters' spidery spare bedroom, on a hard, uncomfortable bed that made his bottom sore, he woke up in a very bad mood. He decided to play a trick on the two witches. He entered the bathroom, next to his bedroom, looking furtively around him. He turned the cold water tap on. He hated hot water! Then, he crept back into his bedroom and went back to sleep, forgetting to turn the tap off.

The sisters were in the kitchen. Frieda was working on a new magic dance potion for her and Oily, while Hattie was preparing a large Austrian breakfast, for she knew that the ugly creature would be hungry. The treat in store for Oily consisted of ham, bacon, boiled eggs, orange juice, followed by coffee and cake. It was the sharp-eared Hattie who heard the sound of running water.

"Frieda! Ich kann Wasser hören!" ("Frieda! I can hear water!")

"Wasser? Es ist dieser Dummkopf!" ("Water? It is that idiot!")

The sisters raced upstairs and found Oily stretched over the bed, snoring his ugly head off. Hattie ran into the bathroom and turned off the running tap. She was just about in time. The bath was beginning to overflow with cold water. She returned with an evil smile on her thin face. She whispered to her sister, who grinned. Chuckling away, like two silly schoolgirls, the sisters managed to lift him off the bed. Struggling to the bathroom because he was so fat and heavy, they gave a mighty heave and sent him flying into the cold water. The result was electrifying. Oily gurgled and gasped. The shock of meeting cold water made him instantly wake up. He spluttered and yelled. Hattie laughing, threw him a flannel and a bar of soap.

"You now must vash yourself mit soap und zen, ven you are clean, meine gut sister here vill bring to you your new cloze for der dance."

Oily was raging. He tried to scramble out of the bath, but each time he tried to grasp the iron rail, it gave him a shock and he fell back in the water, cursing and screaming. The sisters then left the bathroom, locking the door behind them.

"Ven you are clean, you bang on ze floor und I vill come up and give you your new cloze. Is gut, ja?" a giggling Frieda told him.

"No! It ain't good. Potty German witches! Just youse wait and see," he gurgled.

"Wir sind keiner Deutschen! Wir sind Osterreicher!" ("We are not German! We are Austrian!") Hattie shouted at him, through the locked door.

Oily had to do what the witches wanted. He took off his old smelly clothes, trying to avoid the soap and sponge. Unfortunately for Oily, both were magical, so, together they washed and cleaned him, until not a dirty stain nor stink remained. Only then was he allowed to get out of the bath. He was still very wet, cold and angry.

Frieda had kindly left a large green towel for him. This, too, was magical and it dried every inch of him. He was now dry and clean. He banged on the floor. Frieda ran back upstairs and opened the bathroom door. There stood her so-called boyfriend, clean and shining, the bath towel around his vast waist. The glare he gave her would have made lesser women run, but Frieda was made of sterner stuff and, anyway, she found the whole situation rather funny.

"Danke schone, Oily ("Thank you, Oily"). You ae looking zo clean und fresh, zo ven you puts on ze cloze zat I hef put out for you, ve vill vin zis competition and all ze uzzers zat you do not like vill votch in vonder, ja – und me und you, ve make zem zo very jealous."

Her remarks softened his mood. "It better 'ad then," he snorted.

One odd thing about Oily was that despite his dislike

of bathing, he loved to dress up. This is partly because he saw himself as classy, but also, so he believed, to attract pretty young things like Su Fa Su Gut and her faerie and elf friends. This had not yet happened and unless his 'witch girlfriend' were to cast a rather dark spell over Su Fa, it was never going to happen.

Oily admired himself in the cracked mirror, which was the only other piece of furniture in the sisters' spare room, apart from the very hard bed. He was wearing a black dinner suit with a shining, silver shirt and a golden bow. The reflection smiled back at him.

"Youse duzzent arf look 'andsome," it lied to him.

When he presented himself in their kitchen, Frieda exclaimed, "Mein Gott, Oily, for vonce you look zo smart."

Oily smirked. "Yeh, ain't Oi?"

"Zo, don't go spoiling it by putting all mein Früschtück ("my breakfast") over it, ja!" Hattie added. But for once, Oily ignored her nasty remarks. He tucked in and, remarkably, did not spill any of the delicious bacon, ham, cheese and eggs, nor the coffee and cake. His manners were still awful. He gobbled all his food and gurgled down the orange juice and coffee, but that was as bad as it got.

After the huge Austrian breakfast, Frieda went to get ready. When she returned to the kitchen, looking every bit a beauty in a dark blue flowing dress, with a green ribbon holding up her golden plaits, even Oily passed a comment.

"Youse'll do," he remarked and Frieda smiled.

Hattie did not. She was dressed in a black tunic with a flat brown hat on her head. But then, she was not going there to dance, only to win!

The three set off on the short walk to the part of the woods where the competition was taking place. It was almost eleven and the dancing was due to begin at midday.

There was not yet a large crowd. The good folk of Smelly-Welly were not early risers. The three judges and all the other dancers were already there. The astonished stares, whispers and giggles that Oily and Frieda received from the other dancers were nothing to the expressions of horror on the faces of the three judges: Ho Ho He, Madame Popeen Propaire and Tru Lee Loverlee, who was Su Fa Su Gut's best friend.

"'E cannot dance, 'ere, why you breeng 'im viz you?" asked the unhappy French faerie.

"'E can't dance at all, never mind 'ere," exclaimed Ho Ho He.

Tru Lee Loverlee said nothing, but shook her pretty head in agreement. Frieda was having none of it and she was backed up by her scary sister this time. All the folk, including Madame Popeen Propaire, who was quite a strong lady herself, were more than a bit frightened of the once-great Viennese witch and her legendary powers of dark magic.

"Oily ist mein partner, and viz him, I am dancing, ja," she informed the three judges.

"Non! C'est impossible!" ("No! This is impossible!") shouted Madame Popeen Propaire. "You ef not put een your names!"

"That be right. Yer all too late. So sorry an' that, but goodbye," grinned Ho Ho He.

If the judges thought that was the end of the matter, they were so mistaken. Hattie came up to Ho Ho He and, staring him right in the face, said, "Zo, ve hef here zree judges who do not like Oily, von of vitch is a friend of Su Fa and ze uzzer, if I am not mistaken, is Grizzelgut's friend – and as zey boze dance here today, how do ve know zat you vill not vote for zem, even if zey danz badly, ja?"

"'Ow dare you suggest such a zing," began Madame Popeen Propaire, but she got no further.

"Sorry Madame Pee, but I think we be 'avin' a problem 'ere," groaned Ho Ho He, who guessed where Hattie was going with this.

"Oh ja, ve hef ein problem here. But zis is vot I zink. You let meine sister und der ugly von danz und ve say nozzing – zat all ze judges hef zeir favourites!"

The three judges looked at each other. They shrugged their shoulders and, sighing, a scowling French faerie gave Frieda a form to fill and that was that.

By now, the crowds were beginning to gather, and before long the enchanted wood was thronged by hundreds of elves, imps, faeries, goblins and their hosts, the witches and warlocks, who were running the show. This was how it always was. The witches organised the dancing; the other clans made up the judges. It was a hot day again and there were many folk selling all kinds of food and drink. This time, Hattie was not one of them. She had deserted her cooking skills to watch her sister waltz into Vienna with just her at her side – or so she thought.

The crowd was now at fever pitch. The woodland was so packed with swaying folk that the judges struggled, all clutching their notebooks, to get to their old oak bench, with matching elm table, in the large clearing, which acted as the dance floor. The goblins, possibly the most hard-working clan of all, had erected a special stage, where usually a band of elves and faeries would play their various instruments.

This year, however, being the one hundred and fiftieth anniversary, was not only different, but special. As always, a large golden cup stood proudly on the elm table, waiting to be picked up by the winning couple. But that was not all. To celebrate this special occasion, the witches and warlocks had invited over a leading magical waltzing orchestra from Vienna itself. It consisted of a mix of all clans and the conductor was an elderly elf, known as Herr Von Grabbengroupper.

Ho Ho He, dressed smartly in a red suit, had appointed himself as Head Judge. Looking smug and self-important, he addressed the crowd through a large megaphone. He was not aware of the giggles and crude jokes among the young elves and witches, who thought him a pompous ass.

"Good a'ternoon, good folk o' Smelly-Welly. Terday, as we all know, be very spec—"

"Get on wiv it, ye silly ole goblin," shrieked the voice of one teenage witch.

"Yeh, right, we ain't coom to 'ear ye, we coom to watch the dance an' see our friends, Kathy and Selina, win, see," yelled another.

"I ain't goin' to be stopped by a bunch o' youn' witches wot think they—"

But he was stopped. Not by the 'youn' witches', but by a rather large French faerie, who snatched the megaphone from him. He glared at her but sat down again.

"Bonjour, mes amis," she began. ("Good day, my friends.") "Today iz, az we all know, special. Zere iz· not only zis great orchestra 'ere from Vienna, but for ze winners, a special prize zat we will announce when we know 'oo zey are. First, ze couples. Zey are: Greezzelguts and 'is partner, Scrumbletops, for ze gobleens. Next, we ef Crimpy Crackpot and 'is partner, Penny Piper, for ze imps. Zen comes ze pretty elf Zu Far Zu Gut, wiz 'er boyfriend, Emmerod, for bose elves and faeries. Also, we ef Caramel Cathy an' 'er friend, Selina Snakebite, dancing for ze witches…"

Madame Popeen Propaire had to stop because of the loud cheering from all the teenage witches' friends. She smiled and politely waited before continuing "… and lastly, an' I am meaning lastly, we 'ef a late entry. Frieda 'Asbug an'… an'…" – here, she appeared to choke – "an' 'er partner, Meestah Gasbag. I do not know 'oo zey represent."

She was quickly told. "Zey are representing der House of Hasbug, von of Vienna's greatest houses," the haughty Hattie informed her.

Madame Popeen Propaire sniffed. "Zere are four dances. Zey are: polka, quickstep, folk and, finally, ze waltz."

Oily glared at Frieda. "Youse didn't say nuffink about no folk dance!"

"I did not know zis! No matter, ve still vin zru!"

"Better 'ad, an' all."

Madame Popeen Propaire cleared her throat and continued, "Zis is 'ow it works, non! All ze contestants dance togezzer an' after each dance, ze judges make votes – an' ze couple wiz the lowest score, well, c'est au revoir ("it is goodbye")! Whoever is ze last couple will be declared ze winner."

The French faerie nodded to the dancing couples to take their places. She then gave the signal to the conductor of the orchestra. Herr Von Grabbengroupper raised his baton, clicked his heels in salute and the orchestra began to play a fast Strauss polka.

Oily surprised himself. With Frieda barking instructions at him and leading, the two of them put on a spellbinding show, which is exactly what it was. The other four couples were simply left standing. Old Grizzelguts and his daft partner, Scrumbletops, were so bedazzled that they forgot to dance at all. The judges, including a very unhappy Ho Ho He, had no choice but to vote them off. Now there were four.

The next dance was the foxtrot, and again Frieda and Oily were the perfect couple. Not one step did they put wrong. The crowd – who, at first, had been very upset to see Oily there – were beginning to warm to him and Frieda. Indeed, many liked the mischievous Austrian witch and if she wanted to be with that large, ugly fool, then so what? This time around, Crimpy Crackpot accidently kicked Penny Piper, who promptly hit him, then left the stage with much laughter ringing in her ears.

The couples were down to three: Oily and Frieda, Cathy and Selina, and Su Fa and her handsome Faerie boyfriend, Emmerod, at whom Oily was glaring. The Viennese orchestra was playing a very catchy Austrian folk dance, but there was a problem and it loomed large. Here, all three couples had to swap partners, and despite Frieda's attempts to transform herself and the clumsy Oily into ballroom champions, she had given no thought about him dancing with pretty elves or, worse, young teenage witches!

As the fast folk music began, all three couples were swirling around each other and it was difficult to see who the best dancers were. That all changed when the partners swapped. The men had to stand still and the ladies had to move on to the next partner. Oily's eyes glittered with joy as the beautiful Su Fa Su Gut glided sweetly towards him. He was supposed to hold hands and dance up and down, as each couple took it in turns. But Oily was not going to let this chance of dancing with the real love of his life pass him by. He went to grab the startled elf by the waist and, for a moment, it looked like all would end in disaster for Oily and a very jealous and upset-looking Frieda. But as he tried to grab her waist, the lithesome elf stepped back and managed to take his hands in hers, so that Oily found himself dancing around the other couples in an instant. It all happened so fast that apart from Oily, Frieda and Su Fa, no one else had any idea of what that stupid oaf was trying to do.

The next female to dance with Oily, however, was not as graceful as Su Fa had been, and had magic of her own to play. Caramel Cathy squeezed Oily's hands hard and as they danced around the others, she stuck an invisible pin into his left hand, with a wicked smile on her cheeky face.

"Ye an' that dopey witch ain't gonna stop me an' me friend from winnin' this cup, see, Mistah Fatbug," she whispered to him. Neither Hasbug sister had expected that. Oily yelled as the pin hurt him and lost control.

"Oi'll shows yer, yer nasty little witch," he screamed at her, and he broke away and started to chase her around the woodlands, much to the dismay of the sisters but to the delight of the crowd, who were growing a bit bored. Unlike Oily, Caramel

Cathy was fast on her feet and she dodged around the other dancers as the clumsy creature went after her. He sent Frieda flying and Su Fa Su Gut ran off the stage in fright. Emmerod tried to stop him, but Oily pushed him out of the way.

"Come 'ere, youse 'orrible little gayl," he yelled. "Oi'm gonna get youse!"

"Coom an' catch me if ye can, silly ole Mistah Gobbag," she cackled and started to run circles around Oily.

The orchestra was still playing, being from Vienna, as if nothing had happened. Oily was going bonkers. Caramel Cathy was having the time of her young life and, loudly cheered on by her gang of young teen witches, was about to jump on the stage when Hattie shouted, "Halte jetzt!" ("Stop now!") She was so angry, she forgot she was not yet back in her beloved Vienna.

Herr Von Grabbengroupper stopped conducting, as if struck by lightning. Everyone stopped, even Caramel Cathy and her friends, and Oily, too. Hattie was about to continue in those harsh tones of hers and explain to a wondering and mystified crowd why she had uttered that command, but Madame Popeen Propaire stuck her upturned nose in first.

"Zis is a disgrace. You 'orribly fat cochon ("pig")! Again, you ruin our dance! You chase zis pauvre jeune sorcière ("poor young witch") around ze dance and zo, you go out. Zat is you an' zat silly witch, Frieda. Zis is our decision."

In truth, in was not. It was hers alone. That is not to say that Ho Ho He and Truly did not agree; they did, but Ho Ho He, especially, would have liked to have spoken, despite wanting Oily and Frieda out.

"Ich denke nicht!" ("I think not!") The harsh tones of Hattie Hasbug rang out loud and clear. She stormed onto the stage, grabbed the astonished Caramel Cathy by her ear and led her back into the centre of the dance floor, yelling and spitting.

"Leave me alone, ye ugly ole German witch," she screamed, showing her ignorance.

Hattie just ignored her. She let go of her ear and transferred her grip to the young witch's left hand. She shook it vigorously and pointed it downwards, and from her pretty sleeved dress a number of large, coloured pins dropped out and fell to the floor. There were gasps of horror from the crowd. Hattie then marched the now-woeful looking young witch to Madame Popeen Propaire.

"Zis iv vy zat dopey dummkopf did vot he did. I do not like him, but he is dancing mit mein sister, zo I am vonting zem to vin, ja – and zis dumme kleine Hexe ("silly little witch") makes mit pin, a pain, for him, so I am zinking, she und her friend are ze vons to go, ja?"

The large French faerie was looking for support from the crowd. She was desperate for Oily to be chucked off. But just for once, the sympathy of the crowd was with Frieda and Oily. They booed the two young, ashamed and sorrowful teen witches. With heads bowed, the duo left the dance floor. Hattie had won, again! Madame Popeen Propaire had now been outsmarted twice by the dark Austrian witch, whom she now hated even more than Oily. She was determined that Su Fa and Emmerod would win the last dance, which was the waltz, and thus the competition.

Frieda glared at Oily, as he went to grasp her waist. "You vont to vin or not?" she growled.

"Course, Oi does, youse daft—"

"Zen you not make mit der look at zat elf girl, verstehen Sie?" ("you understand?")

"Speaks Ingerlish, yer silly ole…" Oily was still hurting from that pin and was in no mood to listen to Frieda.

"I am speaking English, you stupid idiot," she snapped.

"No, youse ain't! Wot do 'fay stashun' mean, then?"

"Means 'you understand?'"

"Don't care no more, see. Got rid of them enemies of mine and if Su Fa wins that silly gold cup, then so wot? Oi fink—" He got no further.

"Ze prize iz an all-paid trip to Vienna!" she told him.

"Oh, youse never told me that before! Well, yeh, fancy a trip to Germany? Yer, orrite then."

"Not Germany, dummkopf! Vienna is the capital of Austria und is full of music, great food und—"

"Alright. Shut yer mouf and let's win!"

Frieda breathed deeply and just managed not to kick Oily in the shins. She composed herself, smiled at the impatient and frowning French faerie, who gave the signal to the relieved Austrian conductor. He raised his baton once more and the beautiful song 'Vienna, City of My Dreams' filled the woodlands with its wonderful harmony.

The two remaining couples danced against each other. It was wonderful to watch. Su Fa Su Gut and Emmerod were very good. They were the perfect couple; always in step and they didn't put a foot wrong. As good as they were, Oily and Frieda were better. The magic was working. As the beautiful song came to an end, Frieda whispered to Oily to sweep her off her feet in one last dance of defiance. Against all the odds, he did. The dance ended. The judges tried their best – well, two of them did – to give more votes to Su Fa Su Gut, but strangely enough it was the quietly spoken Tru Lee Loverlee who won it for Frieda and Oily.

"I know that Su Fa is a very good friend of mine, as is Emmerod. But I am sure you will all agree with me that as good as they were, Frieda and Oily were amazing. So, I am awarding them top marks, ten out of ten, and I declare them this year's winners."

Huge cheering broke out; even Su Fa was clapping and she gave the blushing Oily a smile – something he would cherish for the rest of his life.

Madame Popeen Propaire was not a happy faerie, but she was a polished professional. Reluctantly, she handed the golden cup to a deliriously happy Frieda and then informed the crowd about the grand prize of a trip to Vienna. The crowd gasped.

"'Oo's gonna let them Austrians know about Oily then?" shouted Grizzelguts to much laughter.

"Novon. He is not going. I am going to Vienna mit mein sister!"

There was stunned silence. It was broken by Oily. "Oi ain't 'avin that, youse crafty old Orstrine witch. It were me an' Frieda wot won, fair and square, see, and none of yer dark mag—"

Frieda quickly broke in. "Vy don't ve all go, ja?" She only just prevented her sister and Oily from telling the entire village about how they really won.

"I am meaning zat mein gut sister, here, cooked all ze meals und she has been telling you about ze uzzer cheats, ja?"

The three judges were silent. They did not know what to do. It was the crowd, again, that won the day for Oily, Frieda… and Hattie. They roared their approval. So, it was settled, much to Frieda's delight and Hattie's despair. Oily was, for the first time ever, going to travel to another country. What the Viennese, being so prim and proper, would make of Oily? And what he would make of them – well, that is another story!

THE END

ENDE

LA FIN

Translation Glossary

FRENCH TO ENGLISH

French: La Petite Boutique
English: The Little Fashion Shop

French: "Vous! Quitte ma boutique, maintenant!"
English: "You! Get out of my shop, now!"

French: "comprenez vous?"
English: "do you understand?"

French: "Imbecile! C'est moi!"
English: "Idiot! It is me!"

French: "s'il vous plaît"
English: "if you please"

French: "Jamais! Allez!"
English: "Never! Go!"

French: "Non! C'est impossible!"
English: "No! It is impossible!"

French: "Bonjour, mes amis"
English: "Good day, my friends"

French: "c'est au revoir!"
English: "it is goodbye!"

French: "cochon"
English: "pig"

French: "pauvre jeune sorcière"
English: "poor young witch"

GERMAN TO ENGLISH

German: "sieben Mark, bitte"
English: "seven shillings, please"

German: Die Hexen von Wanderlust
English: The Witches Who Like to Wander

German: deine liebe freundin, ja"
English: "your beautiful girlfriend, yes?"

German: "die jungen Hexen"
English: "the young witches"

German: "machen spass mit Magie"
English: "make fun with magic"

German: "ich denke, ja"
English: "I think, yes"

German: "schlaue Hexe"
English: "clever witch"

German: "Wunderbar!"
English: "Wonderful!"

German: "meinem Besenstiel, nein?"
English: "my broomstick, no?"

German: "mein guter Mann"
English: "my good man"

German: "ja, mein Freund"
English: "yes, my friend"

German: "kommst du mit mir, bitte"
English: "come with me, please"

German: "Warum? Was willst du?"
English: "Why? What do you want?"

German: "Wir haben einen Gast"
English: "We have a guest"

German: "Einen Gast! Wie?"
English: "A guest! Who?"

German: "Est ist mein guter Freund, Oily Gasbag!"
English: "It is my good friend, Oily Gasbag!"

German: "Was? Dieser Dummkopf!"
English: "What? That idiot!"

German: "Er schläfts jetzt?"
English: "He is sleeping now?"

German-: "Stille, bitte!"
English: "Quiet, please!"

German: "Natürlch, ja!"
English: "Of course, yes!"

German: "Das ist gut"
English: "This is good"

German: "Frieda! Ich kann Wasser hören!"
English: "Frieda! I can hear water!"

German: "Wasser? Es ist dieser Dummkopf!"
English: "Water? It is that idiot!"

German: "Wir sind keiner Deutschen! Wir sind Osterreicher!"
English: "We are not German! We are Austrian!"

German: "Danke schone, Oily"
English: "Thank you, Oily"

German: "Halte, jetzt!"
English: "Stop, now!"

German: "Ich denke nicht!"
English: "I think not!"

German: "dumme kleine Hexe"
English: "silly little witch"

German: "verstehen Sie?"
English: "you understand?"